The Tight Rope: God, Help Me
By J. Mike Rollins
Copyright © 2026 Jonathan Micheal Rollins

In this coming-of-age story for young adults, a boy's quiet doubts about God slowly grow into something much darker. Hoping for clarity, he reaches into darkness, and something reaches back. His journey becomes a chilling reminder that some questions demand a price.

CONTENTS

The Graveyard

S haron's voice trembled with excitement as she took her husband's hand. "Mark... we're having a baby boy."

His face lit up. "That's amazing! Have you thought about names yet?"

Sharon nodded, a smile spreading across her face. She whispered, "Timmy."

Mark replied, "I love it."

Mark and Sharon lived at the end of a lonely country road in an old two-bedroom ranch house. With a farm on one side and a church on the other, not many people came down the road except on Sundays. In the mornings they could hear the rooster, the cows, and, on Sundays, the church bells. They hoped to buy a house closer to town, but for now, this was all they could afford.

Mark and Sharon made great efforts preparing for their new child up until the day he was born. Once Timmy arrived, Sharon took a break from her job to care for him. Every morning she walked with him in his stroller. They circled the church and then headed toward the farm. "Hey Timmy, look at the cows." He giggled whenever one mooed. Sunday church was about the only social outlet in that part of the county.

Their daily walk took them behind the church, but never through the graveyard. As she passed the gate, Sharon kept her eyes fixed straight ahead, refusing to glance at the crooked headstones that loomed at the edge of her vision. Her hands tightened on the stroller until shrubs and flowers blocked the eerie view. Only then did she finally relax her grip.

One morning, a beautiful butterfly landed on the stroller right in front of Timmy. "Hey Timmy, look at the butterfly." Sharon tried to get his attention, but his eyes kept wandering. A thread of unease tightened inside her; something felt off.

As the months passed, she shared her concern with Mark. "Sometimes, it's like Timmy can't see things right in front of him. I'll show him something, and he'll just look away. I'm worried it might be his eyes... or ears. I think we should take him to a doctor."

When Timmy was almost two, she shared her concerns with the local doctor. Sharon explained, "When I'm holding him and talking to him, he looks at me for a moment, then looks away and stares at the ceiling. At the dinner table, he gazes around the room and stares at walls or chairs. Even when we talk to him, he still looks away."

The doctor waved a little red car in front of Timmy, moving it left, right, up, and down to test his tracking. Sharon watched closely and followed with her own eyes. He whispered and snapped his fingers to test his hearing.

Sharon added, "And he also seems to have imaginary friends. He reaches into the air and mumbles like he's playing with someone. Then he'll turn around and giggle at nothing."

"He appears to interact normally for a two-year-old," the doctor said. "His hearing and vision seem good. I don't think he has autism. He may just have a very active imagination."

Sharon sighed with relief.

"A little more social interaction with other children might help," the doctor suggested.

Sharon brought the good news home. "The doctor didn't see anything wrong with Timmy, but said he needs to spend more time around other children."

Mark was relieved. Sharon added, "Let's have a birthday party. We'll do it Sunday after church. I'll invite some of the ladies I used to work with. They can bring their kids."

Mark said, "I'll ask David to bring his son, Andy."

Over the next few days, they invited everyone they knew with children. By Sunday, the house was packed with toys, party favors, and the smell of food drifting through the air.

When church let out at noon, children raced to Mark and Sharon's home. Little footsteps pounded the floors, giggles echoed through the halls, and the house filled with joy.

David arrived at the door. As Sharon opened it, he smiled. "Hi Sharon. I brought Andy over. Hopefully the boys will hit it off."

Sharon asked, "Was your wife able to come?"

David shook his head. "No... she's not feeling well."

Mark and David headed off to the kitchen as Andy and Timmy played in the living room.

Sharon was excited to catch up with old friends. Her face lit up when Beth stepped into the living room. "Oh my goodness, it's great to see you again."

"It's been forever," Beth laughed. "Timmy was just a month old last time I saw you. How are you?"

"I'm doing well," Sharon said warmly. "How's your son, Johnny?"

"He's six now. He's doing great."

"They grow up so fast," Sharon sighed. She watched Timmy play with the other children. "It makes me so happy to see him around other kids."

Sharon confided softly, "He often plays with imaginary friends. I guess because he's not around many children."

"That may not be a bad thing," Beth said.

"The doctor said he just has an active imagination."

Beth watched Timmy closely as he reached his hand out.

"Look at him," Sharon said. "It looks like he's holding someone's hand."

Timmy walked to the end of the hall, sat down, and giggled at the wall.

"That's interesting," Beth murmured. "I know this will sound odd, but... I think your son may have a gift."

Sharon was puzzled. "What do you mean?"

Beth hesitated, lowering her voice. "I don't usually talk about this, but... I've seen it before. I have a friend who can see things... spirits. Talk to them... even touch them. I believe your son may be able to do the same. It's... special."

Sharon forced a smile, but her eyes flicked back to Timmy at the end of the hall.

With a tremor in her voice, Sharon whispered, "No. I don't believe in ghosts. Are you saying my child is playing with spirits... that my house is haunted?"

"Not haunted," Beth said. "But you live beside a graveyard. This area is full of spirits."

Timmy stood alone at the end of the hallway. He reached out his arm, pointed at the wall, and stomped his feet as he giggled.

Beth's face lit up. "It looks like he's enjoying playing with his friends. They must be friendly spirits."

Sharon's heart sank into her stomach as her hands began to shake. She kept herself together long enough to politely excuse herself.

She scanned the crowd and made eye contact with Mark. Sharon escaped to the bedroom and burst into tears. Mark followed her in.

"What's wrong?" Mark asked, alarmed.

"Beth said Timmy was playing with spirits," Sharon cried. "I don't know what to believe. I'm scared."

Mark pulled her into a hug. "The doctor said he just has an active imagination. He'll be fine."

Sharon looked up at him, still shaken.

"Timmy is having so much fun today," Mark said gently. "Let's go back to the party. Forget what Beth said."

As the party ended, Mark and Sharon walked to the porch to say goodbye to the last guests. They sat together as Timmy played in the yard. Sharon was still bothered. "I don't like the idea that Timmy might be playing with spirits."

"There are no ghosts in our house," Mark assured her.

The wind picked up, groaning through the trees. Sharon's eyes were drawn to the headstones, bathed in moonlight. "I want to get out of here—far away from this graveyard."

Sharon took a part-time job in the evenings so they could save for a new home. They stayed by the graveyard for another year before finally moving to a nice two-story house near the school. The new church had no graveyard. Mark and Sharon made new friends, and Timmy played with children in the neighborhood. They no longer worried about imaginary friends.

Except for the occasional financial struggle, they were a typical middle-class, white-picket-fence family.

Many years passed. As Timmy grew up, he wanted to be called Tim.

2

Backyard Camping

August pressed down with its familiar heat as the first days of school arrived. Tim and his best friend, Andy, walked to school every morning, meeting up with Billy in the schoolyard. Billy was a few years younger, but he always tried to keep up with the older boys. All three were members of the local scout troop that was planning a back-to-school camping and rafting trip at the end of August. The boys were thrilled; it would be their first real camping trip. One afternoon, Mark took Tim out to buy a tent for their adventure.

"Dad, this one looks awesome!"

Mark shook his head. "That one's too small. We need something big enough for the four of us."

Tim scanned the aisle and then pointed. "Dad! Here it is."

It was perfect. Mark hesitated. "It's a little more expensive than I thought."

They spent longer at the store than planned and arrived home late, but Tim was determined to set up the tent. He dumped all the pieces in the backyard and started assembling the poles as he announced, "I'm sleeping out here tonight."

Mark called out, "Tim, grab that corner—pull it tight." Tim dropped the poles and helped his father spread out the ground cloth. Mark grinned. "Excited for your first camping trip?"

Before Tim could respond, Sharon called from inside, "Mark, what is this? Come in here, now."

Tim saw his mother standing by the window, holding the receipt from the store. Mark handed Tim the tent poles. "Here, finish the tent. I'll be back in a minute."

Through the open window, Tim heard their muffled voices. His grip tightened as the arguing grew louder. Under his breath, he muttered, "Not again."

He got back to work, figuring out how the parts fit together. He slid the poles through the sleeves and began to raise the tent. But as he pulled the pole out the far side, the arch sagged and collapsed. With a frustrated groan, he sank into the grass and waited for his dad.

A moment later, Mark returned carrying sleeping bags, snacks, and a couple of drinks.

"Why isn't the tent up?" he asked.

His excitement drained, Tim replied, "It fell apart."

"What's wrong?"

Tim hesitated. "I heard yelling in the house."

Reassuringly, Mark said, "We were just talking about some things. Nothing to worry about. I'll help you finish the tent."

Tim reconnected the poles and slid them back into the sleeves. Working together, they had the tent up and staked within minutes.

Tim tossed the sleeping bags inside. "Why did you bring two sleeping bags?"

Mark paused. "Well... I thought I'd test out the new tent too."

He pulled a couple of lawn chairs over to the fire pit and opened a bag of potato chips. While snacking on one, he sprinkled a few into the pit.

"Dad, what are you doing?"

"Hold on, I'm going to show you something." Bending over, he lit a match and held it to a chip. "See? The chips are fried in oil, and oil burns." As the chips flared, Mark added, "Easy way to start a fire. Grab some small sticks so we can keep it going."

As marshmallows toasted over the flames, Mark shared survival tips: cooking with foil, filtering water, and the art of tying knots. Mark demonstrated how to tie a bowline knot. Tim watched closely, trying to match every twist and loop.

As night settled in, Mark looked up at the sky. "Looks like God cut out the lights. Let's get to sleep."

They crawled into the tent. Before zipping it shut, Mark glanced back toward the house. Tim noticed.

"Is Mom still up?" he asked.

"Her light's still on," Mark said softly. "Let's go to sleep."

He zipped the tent closed.

With crickets singing outside and the faint smell of a campfire drifting in the air, Tim drifted off, dreaming about the coming trip.

Tim awoke in complete darkness. Though his eyes were open, he could not see a thing.

"Dad? What time is it?" he whispered.

No answer. Just silence.

Tim reached over to nudge his father but found only an empty sleeping bag. His heart pounding, he searched blindly for the zipper on the tent. Panic flared when he could not find it. Finally, he managed to push his way out into the cool, dim light of early dawn.

He paused, catching his breath. A proud smile spread across his face. "I did it. I made it through the night."

Grabbing the half-eaten bag of chips from the night before, he went inside and sat at the kitchen table, starting an impromptu breakfast of stale chips.

"How was your first night camping?" Sharon asked as she walked in.

"It was awesome! Where's Dad?"

"He came in very early. He went to work." Trying to shift the mood, she added, "Why don't you go get ready for school? I'll make you a real breakfast."

She hugged him and sent him upstairs.

The smell of bacon wafted up as Tim got dressed. He quickly put on clean socks and shoes, grabbed his school bag, and headed downstairs. Sharon had cooked fried eggs, toast, and bacon. He ate quickly, knowing Andy would arrive soon.

A knock sounded, and Andy swung the door open. "Do I smell bacon?" he yelled. He walked straight to the table and snatched a strip from Tim's plate.

Tim rolled his eyes. "Yes. Obviously."

Andy wandered toward the back door. "Thanks for the bacon. Hey, is that your new tent?"

"Yeah. Me and my dad camped out last night."

They stepped outside to inspect it.

Sharon opened the door behind them. "It's getting late! You need to leave for school!"

The boys rushed in, grabbed their bags, and headed out.

Andy nudged Tim. "Camping, breakfast, bacon—things must be great at your house."

They stopped in front of the bookstore a couple of blocks away. Tim peered through the window.

"You ever been in there? They've got a book on camping."

"Cool," Andy said, leaning closer.

Tim's eyes widened. "Oh! Look at that. They have a Halloween section too."

Andy grinned. "That could be fun. Hey, did you hear there are real witches around here?"

Tim blinked. "You mean like broomsticks and black cats?"

"No," Andy said seriously. "Real witches like in magic spells and curses."

Tim swallowed and suddenly bolted. "That's scary! I'll race you to school!"

The school was only a block away, and they sprinted the rest of the way.

3

Camping Trip

Tim made a list of everything he thought he would need for the trip. His mom reminded him he would have to pack a toothbrush and soap. As the list grew longer, his dad reminded him that whatever he brought, he would have to carry on his back for miles. Tim spent hours rearranging his pack, trying to get it just right.

On Friday morning, Tim woke an hour before his alarm.

"I know I'm forgetting something."

He mulled over his list, second-guessing every item. Running through camping scenarios, he rolled out of bed and checked his backpack yet again.

"Two T-shirts, two pairs of shorts, socks…"

In the shower, new worries crept in. "Did I pack soap? How am I supposed to shower outside? Did I pack a towel? Maybe I'll just stay dirty."

While brushing his teeth, Tim panicked again. "I need toothpaste! Oh, and toilet paper!" He pulled the roll from the holder and shoved it into his bag.

As he came downstairs, his mom asked, "Do you have everything ready for the weekend?"

"Yes. I went through my bag again this morning."

"You need to get some things from your dad. Since he's not going, you'll have to take the food and cookware."

Tim stopped in his tracks. "What? Why isn't he going?" He raised his voice. "Dad? Are we still going?"

Mark stepped into the kitchen. "Andy's dad will take you boys. I pulled out the cooking supplies you'll need."

Tim's eyes welled with tears. "Why aren't you going?"

"Your mom and I need to work on some things this weekend."

Tim's stomach lurched. He had been looking forward to this trip for weeks. He grabbed the supplies and stomped upstairs. Finding no space in his pack, he decided he would have to carry the extra bag.

"I'll leave the tent by the door," his father called.

Tim muttered, "Great. Another thing I'll have to carry by myself."

Just then, Andy arrived for their morning walk. Tim grabbed his school bag and walked out without saying goodbye.

Andy's eyes lit up. "Guess what? My dad's going on the camping trip!"

Tim slung his school bag over his shoulder and started toward the sidewalk. Andy continued, "He'll pick us up from school so we don't have to walk home."

Tim kept his eyes on the ground. Trying to fill the silence, Andy asked, "Did you finish packing?"

Grumbling, Tim said, "I had to repack since my dad's not going."

"Why did he back out?"

"I don't know. Shut up about it!" Tim snapped.

They finished the walk in silence.

Andy's father, David, picked them up after school. "Come on, you two. We need to get moving!"

They ran to the car, where Andy's camping gear was already packed. "We'll swing by your house to get your stuff," David said, "then go pick up Billy."

David kept chatting as he drove, "This will be an awesome trip. I used to camp when I was young. I hiked a little at this park, but I never camped here..."

Andy chimed in here and there, but Tim sat quietly, staring out the window.

They pulled into the driveway. Tim rushed inside, grabbed his backpack, and slung it over his shoulder. He threw his dad's food bag across the other shoulder, stumbling under the weight. Coming downstairs, he spotted the tent by the door—another reminder that his dad backed out on this trip. He hauled it outside. While closing the door, he tripped and fell onto the tent.

"Dang it, Dad," he muttered.

David climbed the porch steps. "I'll carry the tent." He took it, then picked up the food bag too. Tim felt a little less alone.

Sharon met them at the car. She handed David a bag. "I baked you all some cookies for the ride."

David smiled and passed it to Andy. Sharon asked quietly, "How have things been?"

"It's been rough," David admitted. "But we'll get through it."

They talked for a moment as Tim and Andy tore into the cookies. When the car pulled away, David said, "Save some for Billy."

At Billy's house, David told the boys, "Go help him grab his stuff."

Billy was hardly prepared. As David honked, Andy and Tim shoved whatever they could find into his backpack. Andy grabbed the pack. Tim snatched his boots. They ran back to the car. Confused by what had just happened, Billy stood at the doorway wondering if he had everything he needed. They shouted for him to hurry. Moments later, the four of them began their adventure.

Talking and joking, they made the hour-long drive to the state park. They met the rest of the scout troop in the parking lot where everyone was making their final preparations. David unloaded the gear. The troop gathered near the trail entrance.

"All right, Scouts," said Jim, the scoutmaster. "This will be an easy, fun camping trip. It's only two miles to the campsite. Keep it clean, no shenanigans, no accidents. Follow me."

The goal for the weekend was simply to practice camping and have fun. The hike was not difficult, but many had packed far too much and were exhausted within the first stretch.

"Is it much farther?" someone groaned.

"Yes, it is!" Andy shouted back.

Tim and his friends were used to walking to school every day; the hike did not bother them. To distract the tired hikers, David began a cadence: "One, two, three, four... one, two, three, four..."

After about thirty minutes, they reached the campsite. Some boys collapsed, but Tim and Andy still had energy to spare. The scoutmaster called the troop together.

"Find a spot, set up your tents, and meet back here in one hour."

The center of camp served as a common area, with logs and stumps arranged around a fire pit.

With the fresh smell of pine and the gentle murmur of the nearby creek, Tim and Andy scoped out the perfect spot for their campsite. Proud that he already knew how to set up the tent, Tim directed Andy and Billy through the process while he looked through the cooking supplies his father had packed: a pot, dehydrated food, spoons, forks, and so on.

He arranged nearby rocks into a fire pit. David stopped by. "Good job." Seeing that Andy and Billy were nearly finished with the tent, he and Tim gathered firewood. Tim found a few dry sticks for kindling, and together they dragged a large branch back to camp.

The troop regrouped in the common area. The scoutmaster called out reminders. "Don't play in the fire. Make sure your fire is out before bed." He went over plans for the next day's rafting trip. "Listen to the guides. Wear your life jackets." He finished with, "It'll be dark in about three hours. Go eat dinner, find your flashlights, and get everything done before nightfall. Be back here at nine tomorrow morning, ready to hike out and go rafting."

Billy filled water jugs from the creek and dragged them back. Tim and Andy started the campfire while David rigged a way to hang the pot over the flames. Tim added the dehydrated rice and beans. David handed him a pack of hotdogs.

"I brought these to add to the mix. Cut them up and toss them in."

The boys kept poking at the fire. Even so, dinner was good despite being seasoned with ashes.

As night settled in, they sat around the fading embers. A cool breeze hinted that summer was almost over. Other campsites still echoed with laughter. Scoutmaster Jim made his rounds. David spread the embers with a stick, and the boys took turns putting out the fire in the traditional way.

Inside the tent, they stumbled over each other before settling into their sleeping bags. As Tim rested, he realized how much he had enjoyed the evening with his friends and with David. His thoughts drifted to home. "I hope Mom and Dad are getting along."

As the crickets sang in the cool night air, he said a silent prayer for his parents and his friends, then drifted off to sleep.

4

Rafting

Tim crawled over Andy, accidentally stepping on Billy as he eased his way out of the tent. Dawn had broken, the air cool and still. A faint flicker of firelight glowed from the common area. Leaving Andy and Billy asleep, Tim wandered toward the warmth. As he approached, he heard the low murmurs of David and Jim.

"Morning," David said.

Still half-asleep, Tim nodded and sat down on a nearby log. The adults sipped their coffee, their voices calm as they discussed the rafting plans. Warmed by the fire and lulled by their steady conversation, Tim drifted in and out.

As the sun crept over the trees, campers began emerging from their tents and filtering toward the fire. Andy and Billy soon joined them. David heated water over the flames while Tim retrieved cocoa mix and breakfast bars from his dad's bag. After breakfast, they prepared for the morning hike.

At nine o'clock, the troop left camp and headed back along the trail. Without their camping gear, the hike was easy. They carried only a change of clothes, a towel, extra shoes—and some didn't bother with even that. At the trail's end, they boarded a bus that would take them to the rafting lodge.

Tim stared out the window, eager for a glimpse of the river. Most of the route consisted of class I and II rapids, with a few areas edging into class III. When the river finally came into view, Tim pressed toward the window.

"I see it! Look!" he yelled.

Billy leaned over him. David announced, "We're here. The lodge is just around the curve." Seconds later, the building and rafts came into sight.

As they exited the bus, the river guides handed out life vests and paddles. The rafts lined the riverbank. Tim and the boys sprinted to claim their raft.

"This one is ours!" they declared, hopping in and pretending to paddle.

A guide walked up. "All right, hop out and let's talk through the plan."

He demonstrated how to hold the paddle, how to row, how to help steer, and, most importantly, how not to fall out. "Listen to me on the water," he said. "Do exactly what I tell you."

The boys pushed the raft to the river's edge and climbed in. David and the guide shoved off, then hopped aboard. They eased into a calm stretch of river to practice paddling and turning.

"All right," the guide said, "I think you've got it. Let's row!"

The ride began gently, with only a few rocks to navigate. As they progressed, the water grew rougher and steering became more intense. Ahead, whitewater churned. Following the guide's shouted commands, they rowed hard.

"Left paddle! Right back paddle!"

They fought to keep the raft straight. Water slammed into them as they blasted through the rapid. They emerged from the turbulence, soaked and exhilarated.

The guide grinned. "Great job, guys! We've got a couple more of those coming."

The river calmed for a few minutes. Then the next rapid came into view.

"This one's a little harder!" the guide yelled. "Paddle hard!"

He steered them away from the rocks, but the raft pulled back toward the center of the river.

Bam! The raft smacked against a rock.

The impact hurled Tim and Andy overboard. Andy clung to the safety line and hauled himself back in. Tim, however, was thrown clear, his paddle spinning away down the rapids.

The river pulled him under, smashing his knee against a rock. The rapids tossed him violently as he fought to stay above the water. His shoe snagged on a rock, yanking him beneath the surface. For a terrifying moment, water filled his nose as he struggled to free himself. The river finally released its grip, and he burst through the surface, gasping for air.

"There he is!" David shouted, throwing a rescue rope.

Tim grabbed the rope but continued drifting. "Help me!" he cried.

The rope tightened with a sharp tug. Tim looked back and saw David, pulling with all his strength. With each heave, Tim drew closer.

David and Andy reached over the raft's side and hauled him aboard. Moments later, the raft broke free of the rock and drifted downstream.

Shaking, bruised, and without his paddle, Tim sat quietly for the rest of the journey. His hands still clenched around the rope.

There were a few more rapids, but none as dramatic. At the end of the course, the scouts pulled their rafts onto the bank. David helped Tim out and onto the bus. The others eyed the bruise swelling on his knee. Tim already knew he would have a story to tell.

Back at the lodge, the group cleaned up and changed clothes. Tim could walk well enough, though the bruise would linger. To ensure a hearty meal at least once that weekend, they stayed for a late lunch before heading back to the park.

Tim managed the two-mile hike back to camp, though slower than before. Scoutmaster Jim approached him and said, "I hear you had an adventure."

Having already practiced, and embellished, his story several times, Tim smoothly recounted his "near-death experience." Andy cut in, "I fell out too," and the boys quickly slipped into a verbal ego battle. Jim simply smiled and walked back to the front of the line.

Back at camp, Tim tied a rope between two trees to make a clothesline, using the knots he learned from his dad. He and his friends hung their drenched clothes to dry. David started a fire to help dry their shoes. Exhausted, most of the troop rested for a couple of hours.

As sunset neared, Billy dragged some water to camp for dinner. They boiled it as before and cooked beans and rice. David warned, "Don't play in the fire this time. We don't want ashes in the food."

After dinner, Jim visited each group, passing out marshmallows for roasting. He spoke with David for a moment.

"How has everything been at home? How's Andy holding up?" Jim asked.

Jim served many roles in the community, including scoutmaster and youth minister at the church where Tim, Andy, and Billy attended. Jim announced, "We'll have a quick devotional before sunrise if you'd like to join us," he added. "If you wake up early, you can come have coffee with us in the morning."

As darkness settled, they spread out the remaining embers of their fire—perfect for slow-roasting marshmallows. The camp, once buzzing with excitement, was quiet now. After dousing the fire, the weary scouts turned in for the night.

Tim lay in the tent thinking about his spill in the river. He was grateful—grateful for his life vest, grateful David had the rope, grateful that his friends pulled him back in. With those thoughts, he closed his eyes and drifted off to sleep.

5

Questions

Early Sunday morning, Tim felt an elbow jab his stomach as David crawled out of the tent. Unable to fall back asleep, Tim followed him out to greet the morning. David was blowing on the coals from last night's fire as a cloud of smoke mushroomed above the pit. A small flame flickered through the haze.

"We have fire!" David declared.

"Good morning, Tim," Jim said as he joined them. He and David added a few pieces of wood to the fire. "Help us out, would you? Bring the pot of water from the campsite so we can get some coffee going."

Tim returned with the pot and a jug of fresh water. Jim laid out a few cups and instant coffee, and he handed Tim a coffee cup.

The three of them sat around the fire, waiting for the water to boil. As the warmth of the fire settled on him, Tim realized how good it felt just to be included—sitting shoulder-to-shoulder with David and Jim.

As more scouts wandered over for morning coffee and cocoa, Jim began his improvised devotional. "Nature is the artful handiwork of God," he said. Quoting an old hymn, he continued, "The unwearied sun, from day to day, does his creator's power display..." He contrasted God's creation with Satan's desire to destroy.

"Life is like a trail in the woods," he explained. "God leads us toward eternal life, but Satan tries to make us lose our footing and pull us off the path."

He shared how God had helped him through difficult moments. "One morning, I was hiking. The trail was wet. I slipped, slid down a bank, and called out, 'God, Help me!' Miraculously, I stopped just short of a cliff. It was as if a guardian angel had caught me."

That thought lingered in Tim's mind. *I've never seen a guardian angel. I didn't feel God helping me in the river. When I nearly drowned, it was not God on the other end of the rope—it was David. It wasn't a guardian angel pulling me from the water—it was David and Andy.* Tim looked down at his bruise. *Why didn't God stop me from getting hurt?*

His attention drifted back to Jim. "Since then, I can feel God working in my life daily." Jim kept talking, but Tim's mind wandered.

Soon, the other scouts arrived, and the conversation shifted to breakfast. David, Tim, and the boys headed back to their campsite to build a fire. Billy said, "I want to start the fire this time." Tim let him take over. While Billy prepared the oatmeal, Tim and Andy cleaned up around camp.

After breakfast, they began packing their gear. Tim and Andy took down the tent. David doused the fire and helped them finish. Scoutmaster Jim made his rounds, checking that every site was cleaned properly. When all fires were out, the troop began their trek out of the woods.

On the ride home, Andy and Billy slept, but Tim stared out the window, lost in thought. He replayed their hikes, the long nights, the thrill of the river, and the terror of being swept underwater.

They passed an old country church beside a graveyard. Tim had driven by that graveyard many times, never giving it much thought. But today, the crooked headstones struck him deeply. Life can be short, he realized.

When they pulled into the driveway, Tim jumped out and ran toward the house. His parents met him on the porch.

"Mom! You'll never believe what happened!"

Mark and Tim walked back to the car to help David unload the tent and gear.

As they carried things inside, Tim said, "It was so much fun. I fell out of the raft and got pulled way down the river. I'm lucky I didn't drown."

Sharon's eyes widened, her mouth hanging open. David leaned close and said, "It wasn't that bad. He likes to tell the story." After a few minutes, he left to take Billy home. Tim spent a long while recounting the weekend.

"I wish you could've come with us. What did you and Mom do?"

Mark replied, "We drove around and looked at houses in the country."

Tim froze. Emotion tightened his throat. "Are you serious? You want us to move? We can't move!"

Sharon sighed. "Mark, why did you tell him that? You knew it would upset him."

"Well," Mark said, "it was your idea to look at houses."

Tim looked at his mother with fear, then stomped upstairs. From his room, he could still hear them arguing.

"You know we have to cut expenses," Sharon said. "Why are you making me the bad guy? If you were smarter with money, maybe we could stay here."

Tim shut his door to block out their voices.

An hour later, Mark came upstairs.

"I'm glad you had fun this weekend," he said gently.

Tim looked up but said nothing.

"Don't be mad at your mother. We do need to cut back our expenses. We're not moving. Don't worry about that."

Tim eventually calmed down, though he remained quiet through dinner. That night, he lay in bed overwhelmed by the emotional highs and lows of the weekend.

As always, he said a prayer. But this time it felt hollow.

"God," he whispered, "you seem to let yourself be known to other people... but why not me? If you're really there, please let me know." Quietly, Tim drifted off.

6

Dreams

Sleep did not come easily. As Tim lay in bed, he realized how quickly life could change. He thought about the possibility of moving away from his neighborhood. He thought about the terror he felt when the river swallowed him. The throbbing bruise on his knee reminded him of his own fragility. These thoughts tangled in his subconscious and fueled his dreams as he finally drifted into an uneasy sleep.

"Paddle hard!"

Tim heard the river guide shouting commands. He saw himself back in the raft, panic tightening inside him as he knew exactly what was about to happen. He watched from above as he was hurled overboard.

"Oh no! I'm in the water. Gurgling... can't see... can't breathe... I can't find the rope."

His head burst through the surface. Suddenly, everything was dark and quiet. The water was calm. The raft was gone.

He was alone.

He turned toward the riverbank and saw Jim standing on a rock near the edge. Jim looked across the water as Tim called out for help. But Jim turned away and stepped back onto the bank. Suddenly, Jim's foot slipped. As he started to fall into the river, another man reached out and caught him just in time, pulling him safely to the bank.

Tim kept calling for help, but Jim and the stranger did not look back. They walked away as if they could not hear his cries.

The water surged, swallowing him again. Tim thrashed, desperate, hands clawing for anything. His fingers brushed a rope, but it was slack, lifeless in his grip.

"Help! David! Jim! Anyone!"

Fear twisted into anger. *Why are they ignoring me?*

He looked back once more and saw only Jim, and then Jim vanished into the night. Alone and betrayed, he surrendered to the stream, its cold current wrapping around him as he drifted into darkness.

Monday morning returned him to his ordinary routine. Later that week, Tim confided in Jim after the church service. "Other people seem to feel God's presence, but I don't," he said quietly. "I sometimes wonder if I really believe in Him."

Jim hesitated, then opened up. "I probably shouldn't tell you this... but I doubted God when I was younger. I was wild. I wasted so much money going to clubs and bars."

Tim blinked, surprised.

Jim continued, "One morning, I woke up in a field behind a bar. I had nothing on but a pair of shorts. I was freezing. I had no idea what happened that night."

Tim listened, captivated.

"I had blood on my stomach and arm," Jim said. "I didn't know if I'd been stabbed or if I'd gotten into a fight. Well, it was both. I spent a few days in the hospital. That was rock bottom. I cried out, 'God, help me!' and promised I'd change my life." Jim looked down at his hands. "From that moment on, God helped me clean up."

Tim finally asked, "Do you still... do any of that?"

"Absolutely not," Jim said firmly. "I'm still tempted. Sometimes I remember being at the clubs—the music, the lights—I used to enjoy being tempted by the dancers. But, God helps me stay on the right path. I have no doubt that God is real. I feel His presence every day."

7

History Class

As the seasons began to change, Tim grabbed a light jacket for his walk to school. Andy was not feeling well that day, so Tim walked alone. As usual, he stopped by the bookstore window. Sitting in the display was the camping and survival book he had been eyeing for weeks. He had been saving his allowance and hoped he would have enough money soon.

He picked up his pace and ran the rest of the way. Bounding up the steps, he slipped into History class just before the bell.

"Today we will begin our exploration of the Great Awakening period within the Colonial era," the teacher announced. The class had just finished covering the Salem Witch Trials. "We're going to look at early literature from this period. Jonathan Edwards is known as a key figure, especially for his works in philosophy and theology. Today we'll read one of his revival sermons, 'Sinners in the Hands of an Angry God.'"

As Tim listened, a quiet dread crept in. He knew he would have to write a paper. At this point, the witches of Salem sounded far more interesting to write about than a fire-and-brimstone preacher.

Tim visited the bookstore on his way home. The Halloween section was prominently displayed, rows of books about ghosts and hauntings. "Hey, a book about witches," he muttered. "Maybe I can find something for my History paper."

He wandered further and found a title tucked in the Religion section: *Gods at War: The Battle for the Human Soul.*

Twelve dollars, Tim thought. *I only have ten at home. Maybe I can get an advance on my allowance.*

As he walked toward home, Tim heard a high-pitched squealing. He looked up to see his mother's car turning the corner. The squeal sounded again as she turned into the driveway.

"Hey, Tim! Come help me with the groceries," Sharon called.

Tim grabbed two bags and a gallon of milk. As he set the bags on the counter, the milk slipped from his hands and hit the floor with a loud thump.

"What was that?" Mark yelled from the living room.

"Tim dropped a gallon of milk," Sharon called back.

"He needs to be more careful! We can't be wasting money. Make him clean it up."

"It's all right," Sharon said loudly. "It didn't split open."

Embarrassed, Tim ran up to his room.

He dove into his homework. After reading about Jonathan Edwards for a while, Tim let out a loud sigh. He pushed the book aside and opened his math book. Sharon eventually called up the stairs.

"Time for dinner!"

At the top of the steps, Tim paused, listening. No arguing, at least not right then.

He filled his plate with meatloaf, macaroni and cheese, and coleslaw. As he sat down, his mother asked, "How was school today?"

"It was okay. I have to write a paper for History class. We just read about the Puritans, the Salem Witch Trials, and Jonathan Edwards."

"That sounds interesting," Mark said in a monotone voice.

"Not really. But the witch trials are interesting. I think I'll write about that."

"That sounds interesting," Mark repeated, his voice flat, his eyes fixed on his plate.

Tim turned to his mother. "Can I have an advance on my allowance? I want to buy a book from the bookstore to help with my paper."

"How much does it cost?"

"Twelve dollars, and I only have ten."

"Your father will give you five dollars after dinner."

Sharon added, "The car was making noise again today."

"I heard it squeaking horribly," Tim said. "It sounded awful."

Mark grimaced. "I'll take it to Bob's in the morning. It's probably just the belt."

Sharon replied, "I'd rather you take it to the dealership."

"We can't afford the dealership."

The rest of dinner passed in silence. The only sound was the ticking of the clock on the wall.

When Mark finally stood from the table, he pulled out his wallet, removed a five-dollar bill, and set it in front of Tim without a word.

Research

The next day in History class, Tim stared out the window, daydreaming, when the teacher's voice snapped him back.

"Your papers on the culture, life, or governance of Colonial America are due in four weeks."

Tim let out an audible sigh.

"Use your textbooks and at least two additional sources," she continued. "Don't wait until the last week to find your material. I have books on the shelf in the back if you need extra sources."

After class, Andy lingered as Tim browsed the titles on the teacher's bookshelf. One caught his eye: *Macbeth*. He remembered the witches' opening line: "When shall we three meet again? In thunder, lightning, or in rain?" But now he was excited to learn about real witches rather than Shakespearean ones.

He scanned the shelf. *The Delusion of Satan. The Devil's Snare. Salem Possessed.*

He picked a few books, choosing them mostly by how interesting the titles sounded.

He carried them to the teacher.

"I've written them down. You can keep them for four weeks," she said, making quick notes.

Tim and Andy started their walk home.

As they approached the bookstore, Tim asked, "What are you doing for your report?"

"I don't know yet. Do you?"

"I'm writing about Salem witches. I want to stop in and get that religion book, *Gods at War*."

"That sounds cool."

Tim opened the bookstore door and passed the Halloween display on his way to the Religion section. There it was: *Gods at War: The Battle for the Human Soul.*

He repeated the title aloud and said, "That sounds so cool." He held it up for Andy to see.

Andy was holding a book on witchcraft and spells. "This will be fun for the Halloween party," Andy said.

Tim took his book to the counter to pay.

"Can I borrow two dollars?" Andy asked.

Tim handed him two dollars from his change.

At home, Tim dove immediately into his new books. That evening, he read about Betty and Abigail, two young girls in Salem. Betty, the minister's daughter, shared a room with her cousin. Mischievous and curious, they had dabbled in fortune-telling.

"Abigail, fill the Venus glass halfway with water," Betty said.

Betty placed an egg on the table. "Now we crack it just a little..." She let the egg white drip into the glass. "What do you see?"

Abigail's voice trembled. "It looks like... a coffin."

"That's what I thought too," Betty whispered. "That means we're going to die!"

Panicked, the girls tossed the egg away and ran. That night, they felt a heavy dread—as if someone had cursed them.

Tim paused his reading and went to his dresser. From the bottom drawer, beneath old clothes, he pulled out his Ouija board. He, Andy, and Billy sometimes played with it. He always kept it hidden so his parents could not find it.

He sat back down and continued reading.

"Help me!" Betty shrieked in the night.

Her parents rushed in to find Betty and Abigail writhing in pain.

"What's wrong?" Samuel asked.

"I feel like someone's stabbing me with needles," Betty cried.

"I feel it too," Abigail gasped.

Betty added, "When I woke up, I saw a lady stabbing my leg. When I screamed, she flew out the window!"

Abigail began shaking violently.

"It's Tituba," Betty cried. "She's a witch. She's torturing us!"

Tim placed a pencil on the page to mark his place and closed the cover. *Could witches really do that?* he wondered.

"Dinner's ready!" Sharon called from the kitchen.

Tim grabbed his water glass and went downstairs.

"How was school today?" Mark asked.

"I started my report on the Salem witches."

"Don't you mean the Salem Witch Trials?" Mark corrected.

"It's the same thing."

"I don't think there were any real witches," Mark said. "Just mass hysteria."

Sharon took a sip of her drink. "Or maybe something in the food made them hallucinate."

Tim straightened. "Or maybe it was the devil."

Setting her glass down, Sharon said, "I'm not sure I believe the devil is real."

"If you believe in God, then you have to believe in the devil too. Right?" Tim challenged.

Sharon sighed. "I don't like you reading about witchcraft."

Mark stepped in quickly. "How was Math class?"

9

Teacher Workday

Tim always looked forward to teacher workdays—no homework, just hanging out at Andy's house playing games and watching movies.

He and Andy were about to start a movie when they heard a car pull up to the house.

"Who is that?" Andy walked to the window and peeked out. A strange car was in the driveway. The back door opened, and Billy stepped out.

Andy yelled, "Billy's here!" Tim jumped up and rushed to open the door.

"My sister and her boyfriend drove me over," Billy said as Cindy and her boyfriend, Stephen, walked up the steps behind him.

Stephen said, "Well, don't just stand there. Go on in," as he nudged Billy forward.

Stephen barged into the living room. "You got any beer here?" Without waiting for an answer, Stephen headed into the kitchen. "Jackpot!" he called out. A moment later, he returned with a couple of beers he scored from the refrigerator.

His speech was already a little slurred. "You boys gonna be good for a while?" he asked.

Andy nodded and waved the TV remote. "Oh yeah. We just started the movie."

"Good. Have fun. Cindy and I are going to find a quiet place so we can study." Stephen and Cindy giggled as they slipped upstairs. A moment later, the dull thunk of a door closing echoed from above.

Tim looked at Andy, saying, "He smelled funny."

Andy sighed. "I hope my dad's not counting his beer."

About an hour into the movie, Tim and Andy took a break to grab snacks from the kitchen while Billy ran to the bathroom. A loud bang and a rattle came from upstairs.

"What are they studying up there?" Tim asked.

Andy shrugged. "Must be some sports stuff."

Tim grabbed a couple bags of chips, and Andy carried a few drinks back to the living room.

As the movie ended, Stephen and Cindy came downstairs to find the boys lying on the floor in front of the TV. Andy lifted his head.

"What was that noise up there?" he asked.

Cindy's cheeks flushed. "Sorry. We knocked over your lamp while studying."

Stephen quickly changed the subject. "Hey, I saw your book of spells upstairs. That stuff is kid's play. If you want to know about real spells and black magic, I can show you things that will blow your mind."

Tim and Andy sat up straighter, listening.

"We've got this sick little spot in the woods where we mess around with all kinds of crazy stuff. Way cooler than your kiddie book." Stephen whispered something to Cindy, making her giggle.

"If you're not scared, I'll tell you the secret location where we meet."

The boys' eyes lit up. "Yes!" all three said in unison.

Andy glanced at Billy. "You're too young."

Stephen smirked. "The full moon is next Friday. We meet at our hideout in the woods behind the football field. Just before you get to the lake, you'll see a fire pit and a couple of logs on the left. That's where we'll meet at sunset." He grinned. "That is... if you're not scared."

10

Sunset

It was Friday, and the full moon would rise at dusk. Tim and Andy accepted the challenge to meet with the older students behind the football field that evening.

When the final bell rang, Andy asked, "Can your dad still give me a ride home from the football game?"

"Yeah," Tim said, "but we'll have to leave early. My dad doesn't want to stay for the whole game." Tim was not especially interested in the football game, but going to the game meant he could visit the hideout in the woods and still get a ride home.

"We have time to go to the woods." Tim paused, watching Andy closely. "That is... if you still want to."

Andy grinned. "Let's go."

They lingered in the halls and the library for a while before eventually making their way to the football field.

Players were warming up as they walked behind the stadium. The cross-country team sometimes used this trail, but not today. It was about a five-minute walk from the field to the lake. Tim tightened the straps of his backpack and headed down the path.

"Yuck! I smell a skunk!" Andy exclaimed.

"Yeah, me too. Don't get sprayed. I think we're close to the hideout."

Around the curve, they spotted three guys standing around a fire pit.

Andy whispered, "Look... they're smoking."

Tim stepped off the trail and into the clearing.

"Are you kids lost?" one of the teens asked.

"We're looking for Stephen," Tim said. "He told us we could come over."

"Oh. He's not here yet."

Andy eyed the joint in the boy's hand. Trying to sound cool, he asked, "Is that any good?"

The guy chuckled. "Aren't you a little young to be asking?"

"I'm young. But I'm cool," Andy insisted.

"Stephen said you guys were into witchcraft... or something," Tim added.

"Yeah, dude. We smoke pot, read spells, stuff like that. We come here whenever there's a football game."

Tim noticed an old book resting on a stump. The cover was a burnt red, showing a tormented, winged figure falling from the sky. He bent down and touched the cover.

"Is this... the book?"

"Yeah. You can look at it. But the last few chapters aren't for children. Ha!"

Tim sat on a log and placed the book in front of him. Above the image was the title, written in calligraphy: *Dark Verse: Poetry and Spells of the Occult*. The bottom of the cover added, "A collection of shadowed wisdom and hidden power."

Tim felt that this book might finally answer whether God—or the devil—was real. He thumbed through the pages and quickly found the final chapters.

Not wanting to be left out, Andy asked the guy with the joint, "Can I have a puff?"

"Are you sure you can handle it?"

"Just one puff?"

"Okay," the guy said, handing it over. "But don't slobber on it."

Meanwhile, Tim pulled his notebook from his backpack and began copying some of the poems and spells.

He mumbled the lines under his breath:

"By ink and ash, by root and flame,
I summon truth that bears no name.
Between the veils of night and bone,
Let secrets rise from ash and stone."

After the group finished another joint, one of the guys approached Tim.

"I'm John. You interested in Wicca?"

"What's Wicca?" Tim asked.

John explained, "My mother taught me since I was a child. Wicca is how we celebrate nature—becoming one with it. The first section of that book is Wicca. The middle is Satanism. The last part is more like devil worship. We don't mess with that."

Tim quickly flipped his notebook page to hide the spells he had already copied from the last part of the book.

"I don't really believe in God or Satan," Tim said.

John raised an eyebrow. "You opened the book to the satanic section. If you believe in Satan, you have to believe in God too. Everything comes in pairs. Light and dark. Joy and sorrow. Just because you don't believe in God doesn't mean he isn't real. Same with the devil. I stay away from the dark spells. Once you open the book to those chapters, it can be hard to close."

John walked back to the group for another draw from the joint.

John's words were heavy, but Tim kept reading. He continued copying until his fingers cramped. Leaning in, he read another verse:

"To perform this verse aloud is to awaken the hidden spirit.

That there is a Devil is a thing doubted by none.

When recited beneath the full moon, the boundary between seen and unseen crumbles.

One must accept that knowledge and answers come with a price."

A chill crept up Tim's neck. Instinctively, he slammed the book shut. Eager to leave, he hurried to return the book. It slipped from his hands, landing on the stump with a dull thud. It fell open to the same section he had just read.

"Hey! Be careful with that book!" someone snapped.

Tim was done.

A few more guys had shown up, laughing and smoking. Stephen finally wandered over as the boys were leaving.

"Well, you didn't chicken out after all," he said.

"I looked through the book," Tim replied.

Stephen held out the joint. "You gonna smoke some?"

Tim hesitated. "We have to go meet some friends before the game starts."

Walking back, Andy whispered, "Who else are we meeting?"

Mumbling, Tim said, "Just Dad. I wanted to sound popular."

Tim looked back at Andy. "Why are you walking so slow?"

Andy took a couple of quick steps and stumbled to the ground. "Sorry, I'm lightheaded."

The trail darkened as the sun dipped lower. The lights from the football field guided their way.

"The game starts in fifteen minutes," the announcer boomed over the intercom.

They wandered near the field, watching the cheerleaders leap into the air. Then they made their way to the entrance to wait for Mark.

Mark walked up on them. "It smells like someone's smoking marijuana."

Andy responded quickly, "The teachers warned us that some high school kids smoke. We would never do that." He kept extra distance between Mark and himself.

The score was 13-8 as halftime approached. The three of them headed for the hotdog stand.

"Three chili dogs all the way, please," Mark ordered.

Mark finished his dog on the way to the car. "Don't drop any chili in the car."

When they pulled up to Andy's house, David was sitting on the porch.

Andy sighed. "Looks like my dad is sad again."

David staggered down the steps, beer in hand as he walked over to the car.

"How are you doing?" Mark asked.

With slurred speech, David replied, "It's been almost a year since she left. I still can't believe she's gone."

Andy hopped out and punted a couple of beer cans from the yard as he walked toward the porch.

11

Nightmares

Later that night, Tim drifted off to sleep with clips from the book lingering in his mind. As dreams took hold, the cold air of the woods replaced the comfort of his room. He found himself surrounded by John, Stephen, and the others he had met in the woods. He stood before the fire pit, the old book heavy in his hands.

"Beneath the hollow moon I stand,
With salted flame and open hand.

Between the veils I whisper thee,
Step through the dark and answer me."

He recited these lines in his dream as the others pressed in around him, their eyes fixed on him with unnerving intensity. The fire crackled as a glowing ember jumped from the fire.

John's voice echoed, "This rite must not be spoken lightly. The veil, once opened, does not close so easily."

Sudden darkness fell. The woods vanished, leaving Tim in a cold silence. As he inhaled the stench of the cold night air, a shiver passed through his entire body.

A pillar of smoke arose from the pages. It encircled him like a snake subduing its prey. Its grasp tightened around him—slow, deliberate, merciless. With every breath, the thick smoke spread through his body.

Tim woke coughing, stomach churning, the bitter taste of smoke clinging to his tongue. He tossed and turned for the rest of the night.

As morning approached, the house trembled with thunder. Tim jolted awake as rain hammered against his window. He rubbed his eyes and walked into the kitchen.

"Mom, is it going to rain all day?"

"The weatherman says it might," Sharon replied. "You can finish your History paper today. It's due next week."

That was the last thing he wanted to hear just after waking up. But the storm left him no excuse.

Tim sat at his desk with pen, paper, and notes. He wanted to believe that the devil had landed in Salem and that witches walked the streets. After reading for about an hour, he found a quote from Cotton Mather: "That there is a Devil, is a thing doubted by none."

He paused. He knew that line sounded familiar.

His parents believed the trials were caused by fear and hysteria. To lean his paper in that direction, Tim repurposed another Mather quote: "Since the Devil is come down in great wrath upon us, let not us in our great wrath against one another provide a lodging for him."

Tim wondered if Cotton meant the people of Salem had panicked and overreacted.

Boom!

Tim jumped as thunder rattled the house. The lights blinked out, plunging his room into darkness. He finished his History paper by candlelight. He was not ready to give up his fascination with witchcraft, but he was determined to finish his paper.

He noted that nineteen people had been hanged, and one man crushed to death during the trials.

When he finally wrapped up his paper, the storm drifted away. The lights flickered back to life. Tim looked down. His handwritten notes were scattered across the floor. Kneeling to gather them, he reread the poems he had copied from the spell book.

But one warning caught his eye—one he did not remember writing: "To perform this verse aloud is to awaken the hidden spirit. That there is a Devil, is a thing doubted by none."

He froze. Those were Cotton Mather's words. Yet here they were, in his handwriting, from the book of spells.

Confused and unsettled, he stared at the page, feeling a knot tighten in his stomach. Tim paused, seriously considering that warning.

"Tim," Mark called from downstairs, "come help me clean the branches out of the yard."

Tim put on his shoes and stepped outside. Mist and fog rolled across the yard, littered with sticks and broken limbs left behind by the storm.

"Pick those up and throw them into the woods," Mark instructed.

Tim glanced up and spotted someone walking on the neighbor's roof. "Dad, what is he doing?"

"He's clearing limbs off his roof," Mark said.

"I'd hate to fall off that roof."

"I fell off a roof once," Mark said casually. "The safety rope tightened just before I hit the ground. I'd forgotten I even had it on."

The debris pile grew as daylight faded.

"Dinner's ready," Sharon called.

Tim and Mark washed off the wood stain from their hands and arms before coming inside. Tim mentioned having had a queasy stomach all day. "I thought it was the hot dog from the game, but it still doesn't feel right."

He ate only half his dinner. Skipping dessert, he went upstairs.

"You're still going to church in the morning," Sharon reminded him.

Tim curled into bed and quickly slipped to sleep and to dream.

"Who was she? I saw you with her!" a woman screamed. Her face was blurry, but he could feel her fury.

"I know you're cheating on me!"

Tim realized he was witnessing an argument between a couple he did not know.

"I'm not cheating. Nothing is going on," the man insisted as the woman slapped him across the face.

Tim wondered, *Why am I in their house?* Then he realized he was dreaming.

The scene sharpened. He saw the tears on the woman's face and heard the frustration in the man's voice.

"I warned you what would happen if you ever cheated on me," she said, slapping him again.

"You're crazy! I'm getting out of here!"

The man opened the door and stepped outside.

Bam!

The woman's brother hit him across the face with a baseball bat.

"That's what you get for cheating on my sister!"

The man collapsed. Tim heard a voice scream, "Hit him again! Hit him again!" The brother slammed the bat down repeatedly.

Tim woke drenched in sweat, heart racing. He stumbled downstairs, guided by moonlight. He opened the front door and breathed the cool night air. As crickets chirped, a gentle breeze filled the living room. Grounded in reality again, he whispered, "It was only a dream."

His stomach growled. Remembering the ice cream in the freezer, he scooped a huge bowl of chocolate brownie ice cream. The chocolate overload quickly calmed his startled spirit.

Dong, the clock sounded.

It was one o'clock in the morning.

He went back upstairs to try to sleep again.

"What are we going to do with him?" a woman's voice cut through the darkness.

"I don't know," the man said. "Let's put him in the truck and dump him in the woods." Tim was startled that these were the same voices as before.

"Grab his arm and drag him over to the truck." The raspy sound of the gravel under the body made Tim cringe with every tug.

"Why did you hit him so many times?" the woman cried.

"I don't know. It was like I heard a voice telling me to."

Tim felt butterflies in his stomach as he had heard those voices too.

"Open the door. Let's pull him in."

They barely managed to slide the man's body onto the bench seat.

The truck sped off into the night. The woman hurried to her car and followed close behind.

A moment later, an old tattered red barn appeared in his vision. Tim thought, *I recognize that old barn.*

Tim knew he had been down this road before.

Suddenly, the old truck sped past the barn.

"Where did that come from?"

He knew he was dreaming again. The truck faded away as the fog rolled in.

Then Tim found himself standing in the middle of a gravel road. Dim headlights peeked through the dense fog. He was frozen with fear as the headlights grew bigger and brighter.

Coming into view, the truck barreled down the hill with its headlights focused on him. Unable to run, he heard the ripping of the gravel as the truck slid to a stop, inches from his legs.

The fog cleared. Tim turned around to see the curve in the road. He recognized this sharp curve as it had claimed many cars over the years.

A voice whispered, "Roll the truck down the hill into the gully. It'll be a long time before anyone finds him. It'll look like another accident."

The headlights faded into darkness, and Tim fell into a heavy, dreamless sleep.

12

Daydream

Sunday morning, Tim counted each step as he plodded up the old red brick stairs of the community church. Sunlight spilled across the stained-glass cross set into the tall, gothic windows beside the heavy wooden doors. For a moment, he imagined that this must be what old Salem had felt like.

The church bell rang out as he opened the door.

"Good morning," Jim said as he bustled out of the sanctuary, hurrying down the hallway to teach his class. Mark held the door as Tim and Sharon stepped inside. One of the ladies in the foyer leaned toward Sharon and whispered, "Did you hear about Pam? Oh, I'll tell you later."

Tim followed Jim down the hall while Mark and Sharon joined a few other couples shuffling their way into the sanctuary.

On the way to the classroom, Tim said, "I finished my History paper."

"Did you find any witches in old Salem?" Jim asked with a grin.

"No, just a bunch of panic."

Jim nodded. "Did you consider ergot poisoning?"

"No. My mom mentioned something like that, but I was more interested in witchcraft."

Jim repeated the word slowly. "Witchcraft?" He raised an eyebrow as he opened the classroom door.

Jim began the class. "Today we will review the temptation of Jesus Christ. If you have your Bible, turn to Matthew chapter four. 'Then Jesus was led by the Spirit into the wilderness to be tempted by the devil...'"

Tim's mind wandered. He imagined the devil stalking Jesus through the wilderness as Jim continued reading.

"Are you hungry?" the devil asked. "Let me help you. Here, have a piece of bread. It smells wonderful, doesn't it?"

The voice was friendly yet dripping with deception.

Then he taunted, "If you are truly the Son of God, then surely nothing can harm you. Prove it to me. Let's see if your father can protect you."

His blood-red eyes burned like embers, fixed on Jesus with cold calculation as his persuasive words pressured him. Hearing those words coming from the forked tongue of the eerie, blood-stained creature caused his heart to skip a beat.

Jesus rose up and cast the devil aside, "Be gone, Satan!"

The towering figure of Satan shrank as it faded off into the distance.

As Jesus turned away, his tearful gaze landed directly on Tim.

Jim closed his Bible with a loud thump.

Startled, Tim's wilderness scene quickly dissolved, replaced by the white concrete walls of the classroom.

Jim concluded, "The devil is a great tempter and may try to lure you through your weaknesses or doubts."

As the students filtered out, Tim hung back.

"Jim," he said quietly, "I think I did something bad."

"Oh? Would you like to talk about it?" Jim asked, his tone gentle.

"A guy at school let me look at a book of spells and rituals. They were... pretty intense."

"You're not the first teenager tempted by the mystery of spells and rituals," Jim said.

"Can God forgive me?"

"Of course. There were things I did when I was younger that I'm not proud of. God forgave me. He can forgive you too."

Tim and Jim walked together into the sanctuary as people settled in for the sermon.

Tim wrestled with his thoughts through the entire service. He still was not sure if he even believed in God or the devil. The sermon ended with, "Guide, guard, and direct us all. Amen."

As the congregation filed out, Sharon's friend reappeared and said, "Let me tell you about Pam..."

Tim drifted over to speak with Billy.

All the way home, Sharon talked about Pam's situation. "You will not believe this. Her husband was cheating on her. He said he was going to live with his girlfriend and never come back. He took off in his truck last night. I never thought he'd cheat. He was such a good guy. She loved him so much. She is devastated. Thank goodness her brother is there to help her. Can you believe that?"

Over the next few nights, Tim slept better. The tapping of the rain on the roof lulled him to sleep, and his strange dreams faded away.

13

News

The phone rang. It was a call from Betty.

"Oh! My goodness. Really?" Sharon said in disbelief. "Okay. I'll watch the news tonight."

She hung up and called out, "Tim, help me set the table for dinner." They heard Mark pulling into the garage.

Tim placed plates, forks, and knives on the table. Mark came in, closed his umbrella, and leaned it in the corner. As they sat down,

Sharon said, "We're going to have to watch the news tonight. The sheriff found Pam's husband, Allen. He's dead."

"How did that happen?" Mark asked.

"Betty didn't know. We'll have to watch the news."

Excited to share good news, Tim said, "Dad, I made an A on my History report. The teacher was really impressed with some of the quotes I found."

Mark's face brightened. "Congratulations. You can have a second helping of dessert tonight."

After dinner, Mark and Sharon relaxed in the living room and turned on the Channel 13 newscast. Tim scooped out his second helping of chocolate brownie ice cream, his favorite.

In a somber tone, the reporter began, "Breaking news this dreary Thursday evening. I'm sad to report that the Old Barn Curve has claimed another life. Allen Smith was found dead in his truck at the bottom of the gully. Investigators say he was not wearing a seatbelt. This marks the third accident on the curve this year."

A picture of Allen flashed on-screen.

Crash!

Tim dropped his ice cream bowl onto the floor.

Sharon turned just in time to see sheer terror sweep across his face.

"I've seen him before!" Tim exclaimed. He realized it was the man from his dream.

Sharon tried to calm him. "Sure you have. He goes to our church. I didn't think you knew him that well."

Tim forced himself to downplay it. "Oh. I don't. I just... didn't expect to see him on TV."

He cleaned the mess from the floor as the reporter continued.

"We are here with Allen's wife, Pamela Smith. Pamela, when did you last see your husband?"

"He left in the middle of Saturday night. I haven't heard from him since."

Recognizing that voice, Tim looked up and whispered to himself, "That is the woman I saw."

His heart raced. Tim's legs weakened. He started to shake. He sat down at the table trying to calm himself. Mark and Sharon did not notice his reaction as their eyes were fixed on the news report.

Tim replayed flashes from his dream: the baseball bat, the sound of gravel, the rage.

It had not been just a dream. It was Allen.

Pamela continued, "Oh, I loved him so much. I'm glad my brother is here to help me through all of this."

Her brother, Mike, stepped into the frame to comfort her.

Tim's stomach lurched. *That's the man... I saw him...*

With shallow breaths, he cautiously stood, hoping his wobbling legs would support him.

His mom and dad were bickering, "I heard that he was cheating on her."

"Ha! He would never do that. That's just a rumor."

With his heart still racing, Tim slowly made his way up the stairs to his room. As he lay on his bed, he could not believe that his dream was real.

He kept his dream a secret for the next few days—waiting until he could talk to Jim.

Sunday morning, Tim and his parents went to church. After Sunday school, Tim finally confided in Jim.

"Last week, I told you I looked at a book of spells and rituals," Tim said quietly. "Well... I had some strange dreams after that."

Jim grew still. "Okay."

After a tense pause, Tim said, "I saw Allen being murdered in my dream."

"The news said he had an accident," Jim replied gently.

"I saw Mike hit him in the face with a baseball bat. Then Mike and Pam took him to the Old Barn Curve to dump him."

Jim sighed. "Tim... you must have just dreamed about the news story."

"I had that dream last week," Tim insisted. "I saw them murder him."

Jim looked down at his Bible, then at the wall. Taking a deep breath, he said, "Let the Sheriff's office do their investigation." After a moment, he added, "There's no way you can see the details of someone's life in your dreams."

Jim hesitated, as if searching for the right answer... then opened the door and stepped into the hallway. "You need to stop reading that book. Things are hard enough without inviting the devil into your life."

They headed into the sanctuary. Jim took his place on the front row to help with the service. Tim and his family sat, as usual, a few rows behind.

Five minutes into the sermon, Tim struggled to stay awake. The cadence of the preacher's voice eventually lulled him to sleep. Sunlight filtered through the stained-glass windows, draping the sanctuary in shimmering colors.

The preacher's voice faded into rhythmic music.

The squeak of a door echoed from somewhere behind the pulpit. Tim realized he was dreaming again.

"Why is the door opening?" he whispered to himself.

To the left of the pulpit, an arm stretched from the door, finger raised to command attention. The background music pulsed with a dance-club rhythm.

Smoke billowed from the doorway. A woman stepped through the haze, dressed like a dancer from a late-night television show.

Tim's heart raced. "Oh my goodness. I can't believe this is happening in church."

She glided across the stage, tall and graceful.

Tim looked around. "Does anyone else see this?"

Jim followed her with his head. But no one else in the church seemed to notice.

The dancer locked eyes with Jim. Pointing at him, she stepped closer with each beat of the music.

As this graceful and elegant female figure came into focus, Tim saw her clammy, blood stained skin. Her tail curled behind her like a serpent.

"She's a demon," Tim whispered.

She spun around with her tail brushing against Jim's chest. Her cat-like eyes burned like embers as she leaned in and whispered in his ear, "Did you miss me?"

As she looked back, she locked eyes with Tim.

She lingered for a moment as the fragrance of her perfume enveloped them.

Taking a deep breath, Jim folded his arms across his chest and crossed his legs.

Discouraged, she stood up slowly. She smiled at Tim as smoke began to rise around her. With a wink of her fiery eye, she sent a chill down Tim's spine.

Jim whispered, "God, help me."

The music stopped.

An angel appeared between Jim and the demon. As the angel pushed the demon back, the smoke receded. Tim watched as the demon was forced back toward the door.

The smoke slowly faded away.

Tim jolted awake as everyone stood for the invitation song. At the conclusion of the prayer, he walked down the center aisle with the rest of the congregation.

Tim paused for a moment, waiting for Jim. Pulling him aside, Tim asked, "What should I do if I start seeing demons in my dreams?"

Jim sighed. "I don't know much about dreams, but I have dealt with demons." He took a deep breath, letting the preacher mask slip for a moment. "I'll tell you what I do. Whenever I feel the devil is tempting me, I close my eyes and ask God to help me."

Tim spoke little the rest of the day. He tried to convince himself there was no way he could dream about what was happening to someone else.

That evening, Sharon turned on the news.

"New advancements in the death investigation of Allen Smith," the reporter said. "Investigators suspect foul play, as the injuries appear too severe to be caused solely by the wreck. However, storms earlier in the week may have destroyed any physical evidence."

Tim's stomach jumped.

Now he was convinced that what he dreamed actually happened.

14

Temptation

The last week of October had Tim on edge. He usually enjoyed Halloween, but this year the ghosts and demons decorating the halls only fueled his anxiety. That night, the wind, rustling leaves, and wavering moonlight made sleep challenging.

It was the middle of the night.

Click. Thump. Scratch.

At first he thought it was just tree branches against the house, but the sounds came from around his bed. He opened his eyes to a dimly lit room. Light flickered on the walls as though a fire burned somewhere nearby. Smoke clouded the air, and he could barely see across the room. But he could hear voices.

He tried to sit up, but his body would not respond.

A small light appeared above his face. Footsteps circled his bed, accompanied by low whispers and murmurs. He smelled a dirty stench wafting through the room.

A hooded figure leaned over him. Tim saw the glow of light reflecting in blood-red eyes. As the figure lowered his hood, horns cast an eerie shadow across the ceiling. Burned and bloodied skin came into view.

Tim's heart pounded. "I'm seeing demons again."

"This is the one who can see us," the demon whispered. "Unacceptable."

Another demon stepped closer and pulled back his hood. His breath reeked of sulfur. "What shall we do with him?"

A third turned, holding a trident. "We must punish him."

Another leaned over Tim and laid a sword on his stomach. "I can cut him slowly and disembowel him."

A voice in the background shouted, "Burn him!"

Tim was consumed with terror, unable to move or scream.

"We shall meet again," one of them hissed.

The demons faded into the walls. The firelight dimmed to embers. The smoke dissolved.

Suddenly able to move, Tim bolted upright and gasped for breath. He felt his stomach, checking for wounds. Relieved to find none, he lay back down and tried to regain his composure.

Tim barely spoke at breakfast. Forcing a conversation, Sharon asked, "Are you excited about the Halloween party this weekend?"

Conflicted, he said, "A little. Andy and Billy are really excited."

Mark stepped into the kitchen to refill his coffee. Tim asked, "Dad, can we go to the football game with Andy tonight? It's the homecoming game. Can you give us a ride home?"

Tim wanted to speak with John again.

"I will meet you in front of the stadium at 7:30. We can watch the entire game this time," Mark said.

Tim shared the plan with Andy on the walk to school. Andy was excited for the chance to smoke again.

After school, they met Billy behind the building. On their way to the football field, they killed some time by wrestling around on the high jump mat. They played until Billy's dad arrived to pick him up.

Tim and Andy slipped back into the woods.

The smell of marijuana grew stronger as they approached the clearing. Around the bend they saw Stephen and John.

"Hey, the kids are back!" one of the guys shouted. "You ready for some smoke?"

"Bring it on!" Andy said.

Tim walked straight to John. "I need to talk to you."

"Sure, man," John said with smoke drifting from his mouth. "What's up?"

Tim clenched his fists, took a deep breath, and said with a trembling voice, "After I looked at that book, I started seeing demons. And they're doing bad things to people." He hesitated. "Now... they're planning to do something bad to me. I don't know what to do."

John shrugged. "Sorry. But I told you not to read the last part of the book."

"Is there a spell to undo this?" Tim pleaded.

"No," John said. "It doesn't work that way."

Tim kicked at the dirt and muttered a curse word under his breath as he stormed off.

Andy ran to catch up. "Why are you leaving?"

Tim finally told him. "I haven't told you yet, but... I've been seeing demons since we came here last month. I think I'm going crazy."

"Dang, dude!" Andy said. "That sounds cool."

"No," Tim said. "It's scary."

Andy fell silent as they walked back toward the stadium.

The announcer's voice boomed in the distance: "We will begin in thirty minutes. Get your tickets now."

The stadium lights and marching band music guided their way to the front entrance. Mark purchased tickets for the boys, and they paused for the National Anthem.

Homecoming and Halloween falling in the same week made the night feel electric. Games, costumes, crowds—the stadium buzzed with excitement. They bobbed for apples and shared cotton candy before heading to the bleachers.

By halftime, the score was only 14–10. As the marching band entered the field, they headed to the concession stand for some hotdogs. The last half of the game was intense. The final play resulted in victory for the home team. The score rolled 27–24 as the home team roared with celebration. Mark and the boys stopped by the concession stand on their way out to get a couple of discount hotdogs for Andy's dad.

The car pulled into Andy's driveway where beer cans littered the yard.

"How was David doing this morning?" Mark asked.

"He's been sad all week," Andy said.

"Call us if you need help," Mark said quietly.

Andy hopped out, carrying the hotdog bag.

On the way home, Tim asked, "Why is David sad?"

"Well, son, today is the one-year anniversary of his wife passing away."

"Oh," Tim said. "I forgot."

He felt guilty for not remembering.

Later that night, Tim settled into bed thinking about Andy and David. He replayed the camping trip in his mind, especially the quiet morning by the campfire with David drinking coffee.

As sleep overtook him, the image of the fire dimmed and the air thickened with smoke.

Suddenly, he was sitting at a kitchen table with David.

The kitchen smelled musty. Beer bottles littered the sticky tabletop. David picked up a bottle and finished it, slamming it down.

A deep voice spoke, "You need to drown your sorrows. Have another one."

Tim looked around but could not see where the voice came from.

"Here, I'll help you," it continued.

A faint, shadowy arm reached across the table. "Just one more beer."

Tim realized he was witnessing David being tempted by a demon.

The red, scaly demon came fully into view.

"You really miss her, don't you?"

David took a drink.

"I'm sure she meant everything to you."

The demon whispered, "Do you have any whiskey around here?"

The demon walked over to David. "Whiskey will help you forget the pain."

He grabbed David's hand and led him to the pantry.

"There's the bottle. I knew you had some."

David poured some whiskey into a glass, spilling just as much on the table. "Maybe this will do it," he whispered, drinking it all in one gulp.

"That's good," the demon praised. "I'm proud of you."

The demon's tone hardened. "Here, have another one. You don't have anything to lose."

David threw back another, tears streaming down his face.

Then the demon struck deeper. "You failed your son. He's doing drugs. That's your fault. You know that, right?"

"Stop it!" Tim cried. "Why are you doing this?"

The demon slowly turned, eyes blazing. "Shut up, kid! You aren't even supposed to be here!"

He backhanded Tim across the face. Tim flew out of the chair, crashing onto the kitchen floor. His head hit the wall, and everything went dark.

When he opened his eyes, dazed and confused, he heard David sobbing.

As his eyes slowly came back into focus, he could see the table, the demon, and David. A pistol lay between them.

"You've thought about it, haven't you?" the demon coaxed. "That will help you forget her."

David reached for the gun.

In a panic, Tim jolted awake, jumped from his bed, and ran to his parents' room.

"Dad! David's in trouble. We need to go now!"

Mark sat up. "I didn't hear the phone. Did Andy call?"

Tim lied. "I answered it. We need to go right now!"

Mark and Tim sped to Andy's house. Gravel scattered as Mark slammed the brakes. The front door hung open.

Running to the house, Tim shouted, "He's in the kitchen!"

Mark rushed inside with Tim close behind. He peeked around the corner and saw David holding the pistol.

"David," Mark said gently, "put it down. Please. Let's talk. Tell me what's going on."

David hesitated.

"We need you, man," Mark continued. "Don't do this."

David looked at the pistol, breath shaking. Slowly, he set it down and began to cry. "I miss her so much."

The demon rose from the chair. Snarling, he brushed past Tim.

He grabbed Tim by the arm. "Boy, you are going to regret this."

Tim felt a burning pain as a claw broke the skin and blood streamed down his arm. The demon glared at him one last time and walked out the door.

Tim awoke the next morning in Andy's room. He walked downstairs to find Mark asleep on the couch.

"Dad... are you awake?"

"I am now," Mark muttered, sitting up.

They lingered in silence for a moment before Tim asked, "Is David going to be okay?"

"I think so," Mark said. "It may take a day or two."

The kitchen was littered with signs of the night before. Mark wiped the table with a washcloth while Tim picked up the chairs and put them back.

Mark glanced at Tim's arm. "What happened to your arm?"

"Oh. I scratched it last night," Tim said quickly.

Andy wandered in. "I thought I heard you get up."

"Do you have anything to eat?" Tim asked.

Andy found some cereal and milk.

Mark said, "I asked Sharon to come by. She should be here soon. I'll stay with David today, and you two can go with her."

Andy cleaned up and packed for the Halloween party.

As Sharon pulled into the driveway, Tim yelled, "Mom's here!"

Mark and the boys walked outside.

"How is David?" Sharon asked.

"We had a really rough night," Mark said. "I think he's going to be okay. I'm going to stay with him today to make sure."

Mark returned inside as David emerged from the bedroom. "I'm so sorry you had to see me like that," he said.

"I'm just glad Andy called us in time," Mark replied.

They began cleaning the kitchen together and later met up with Jim.

Halloween

Andy and Tim hung out at Tim's house that Saturday.

"We need to pick up Billy for the Halloween party," Tim reminded his mom as they loaded into the car.

They pulled up to Billy's house just as he barreled down the stairs dressed as a ghost, yelling, "Boo! Boo!"

Billy hopped into the car. "What are you going to wear?"

Andy tied a red bandana around his head and slipped a patch over his eye. "I'm a pirate."

"I'm not dressing up this year," Tim said.

When they arrived at the festival, Tim shouted, "Look! They have deep-fried Oreos!" After Sharon parked the car, the three boys jumped out and ran straight to the Oreo stand.

As Sharon joined them, Billy asked, "Can we go in the haunted house?"

"Yeah, can we?" Andy asked.

"I'm not interested," Tim replied.

Andy and Billy ran to the haunted house.

Sharon and Tim met them at the exit a little while later.

"You missed it," Andy said. "That devil scared the snot out of Billy."

Billy shot back, "Well, you screamed when the guy got hanged."

Those were the last images Tim wanted in his head.

That night, as Tim lay in bed, he was glad Halloween was almost over. The weather, however, kept his nerves on edge. Wind rattled the windows, and branches scraped the house with sharp clicks and screeches.

As he drifted off, the eerie sounds outside his window morphed into the clicking of a ratchet and the squeaking of gears.

"Crank it a few more times."

Tim felt his hands being pulled away from his body. He opened his eyes and saw a dark, stone dungeon. He was lying on a table, ropes tied around his wrists, ankles, and chest. With each crank of the ratchet, the ropes tightened, binding him to the rack.

The cold room glowed with firelight, shadows flickering across the walls.

The scaly demon from the night before stepped toward him. "This is what you get for interfering."

The demon opened a box filled with a thousand needles. "This will be slow and painful."

He slid a needle under Tim's thumbnail. Tim screamed! Then his index finger. Then his middle finger. One after another, the demon stabbed needle after needle, sending jolts of unimaginable pain ripping through his body. Tim screamed in agony.

Tim cried out, "Help! They're stabbing me with needles!" His whole body burned. He looked down and saw himself covered with needles.

"I told you that you would regret this," the demon said.

Then everything went black.

Tim regained consciousness in the dream. His body still burned. He looked at his arms and legs and saw bloodstains where the needles had been.

"I want him next," one of the demons snarled. "Let's hang him like the witches in Salem."

"I want to crush him."

Another stepped forward. "Burn him at the stake."

An ash-covered demon leaned over him and locked eyes. In a deep, rumbling voice, he said, "Burning at the stake will prepare you for the eternity you will spend burning in the lake of fire."

"Cut the ropes," the demon ordered. "Drag him to the stake."

The tension around Tim's wrists and ankles released. "Grab his feet."

Each demon grabbed a leg and yanked him off the table. The ropes fell from his hands and feet, but the rope around his chest remained.

Carrying blazing torches, a line of demons marched toward a wooden stake. The smell of burning pitch filled the air.

Tim knew this would be his last moment.

They dragged him over the wood pile and up to the stake. One demon leaned close to his ear and whispered, "This is going to hurt. Ha, ha, ha!"

Ropes cinched around his wrists and feet. Tim's life flashed before his eyes. His doubts about God vanished as he knew he was in the hands of the devil.

He slowly closed his eyes and cried, "God, help me!"

The rope around his chest tightened snugly around him. With a sudden jerk, he was pulled away from the stake.

Tim's mind jumped back to the river, where a rope had pulled him to safety. He looked up now and saw his own guardian angel pulling him from the demon, the stake, and the fire.

Tim realized that the safety rope and the guardian angel had been with him all along. He had simply never called on God for help.

As the angel carried him away, memories flooded his mind.

He saw himself as a toddler by the graveyard, reaching out to invisible friends. They were not imaginary playmates. They were guardian spirits watching over him.

He remembered the camping trip when he felt so alone, not realizing God was there in David's hand as the rope pulled him from the river.

"I was never alone," Tim whispered, tears streaming down his face. "You were always there. I just didn't know how to see you."

Redemption

Tim jerked awake and nearly jumped out of bed.

In a panic, his hands shot to his wrists, then to his ankles, checking for ropes. His eyes scanned the room. *I don't see any demons,* he thought.

The room was quiet.

Tim slowly let out the breath he had been holding and whispered into the darkness, "God... thank you."

His pounding heart started to steady.

The wind stopped howling outside. The branches no longer scraped against the house. A deep calm settled over the room.

He lay back down, reflecting on what had happened.

Tim was quiet at breakfast Sunday morning. He ate slowly, afraid to tell his mom and dad about anything he had experienced.

Sharon sat down at the table. "Tim, how do you like the eggs?"

"They're good," he replied.

Mark took another bite and nodded. "These are great. Where did you get them?"

Sharon smiled. "From the farm where we used to live. Their prices are really good."

She added casually, "We should stop by there again today after church. I want to pick up some greens, carrots, and a few more eggs."

Mark glanced at the clock. "We need to leave for church in about ten minutes if we want to get our seats."

For the first time, Tim climbed the old red brick stairs without the weight of doubt crushing his spirit.

Tim walked to his Sunday school class while his parents headed toward the sanctuary. Jim opened the class by saying, "Let's turn in our Bibles to Ephesians, chapter four."

Tim thumbed through his Bible, looking for Ephesians as Jim began reading.

Tim shivered.

He slowly scanned the room and glanced toward the door.

Through the small window, he saw a shadow pass by. Tim stared as the image came into focus.

It was the demon he had seen dancing in the sanctuary.

With her face pressed against the window, she gazed at Jim for a moment. She winked at him, and then faded back into the shadow.

Jim continued to read verse twenty-seven. "...and do not give the devil a foothold."

Jim paused and looked around the room. "I can't stress this enough," he said firmly. "If you invite the devil into your life, you may spend the rest of your life fighting him."

Suddenly the door squeaked as it slowly opened.

Tim's heart skipped a beat.

Jim looked up and smiled. "Come on in."

Andy stepped inside.

Tim grinned as Andy took the seat beside him.

After class ended, Tim waited in the hallway for Jim.

He hesitated, then said, "Jim, I understand you now. I get it."

Jim studied his face for a moment and smiled. "Well," he said warmly, "that's good to hear."

As they entered the foyer, Jim suddenly spotted David standing quietly near the wall.

Jim greeted him. "I'm glad you and Andy came this morning."

"I want to testify today," David said.

Jim nodded. "I think that would be good."

David and Andy joined Tim and his family in the pew.

As the sermon came to a close, Tim caught a faint musty smell in the air.

He glanced toward the back of the sanctuary.

Out of the corner of his eye he saw an angry demon trudging slowly down the aisle. Tim took a deep breath as his heart began to race.

The towering figure moved slowly and deliberately past each pew until he reached the row in front of them. As he slid down the pew, he turned and glared at Tim, his lip curling in a snarl.

He sat down directly in front of David—between David and the preacher.

The preacher concluded the message. "If you need prayer, if you are struggling with something in your life, we invite you to come to the altar."

As the congregation started singing the invitation hymn, the demon slowly turned toward David. Its stare was cold and relentless.

Tim lowered his songbook as his hands started to tremble.

David rose from the pew and stepped into the center aisle.

The demon followed behind him.

David walked toward the front of the congregation, the demon matching him step-by-step.

When he reached the front, David turned toward the congregation, now face-to-face with the demon.

"This year has been rough," he said, his voice beginning to quiver. "I thank you all for your patience with me."

He took a deep breath. "I want to rededicate my life today."

His voice cracked. "God... help me."

The demon lowered his head.

His shoulders slumped.

The towering figure walked slowly back down the aisle and faded from sight.

On the way home, Mark and Sharon stopped by the farm to pick up eggs and vegetables.

Mark looked around the property and laughed softly. "I don't know why we didn't start coming here sooner."

Mark and Sharon stepped out of the car.

"Tim," Sharon called, "come here for a minute. I want to show you something."

Tim walked over.

Sharon pointed toward a small house across the field. "See that house? We used to live there when you were little. I used to push you in your stroller around the church over there."

She smiled.

"I bet you don't remember that."

Tim looked intently at the house for a moment.

"Yes," he said quietly. "I remember."

Sharon looked surprised. "You do?"

Tim hesitated before speaking again.

"I used to play with the spirits from the graveyard."

Sharon's eyes widened.

"What! No... really?"

Sharon looked away as her face turned pale.

"Oh my... you remember that?"

Sharon paused as tears began to fill her eyes.

She pulled him into a tight hug.

Sharon said, "I am so sorry. I wanted to protect you from that."

Tim spoke softly. "I still see spirits sometimes. But the good ones protect me from the bad ones."

He paused. "I just call on God to help me."

Sharon held him even tighter as she began to cry.

That evening, Tim sat at his desk. Scattered before him were the pages of satanic poetry and spells.

They felt strange now—like relics from someone else's life.

Without hesitation he tore the pages in half and dropped them into the trash.

A shiver of regret passed through him as he realized how close he had come to losing himself.

Later that night, Tim lay in bed.

The house was quiet. No demons lurked in the corners of the room. No flames flickered in the darkness. No howling wind. No tree branches scratching against the walls.

He was finally at peace.

At times, Tim was still the target of the devil. But he no longer faced it with fear. He knew now that he only needed to call on God for help.

As the Psalms say, "Call upon me in the day of trouble; I will deliver you."

And Tim believed.